LIFE ACCORDING TO MATTYIENE

LIFE ACCORDING TO MATTYIENE

COOL BOYS HAVE PROBLEMS TOO!

Malachi Williams

changefactor

Changefactor Limited

1

CHAPTER ONE MY INTRO!

Hi guys! Nice to meet you!

You might think "being cool" means you get loads of friends and that you're the centre of attention at every party. Well, that's only part of the story. There is so much more to being cool! It has its benefits but also disadvantages. In this tale, I will tell you about an 11-year-old Black boy who was so popular, he was like a King at his school.

This popular boy was called Mattyiene. Mattyiene had a flat top. He loved wearing his favourite shirt, with a logo on the front that read 'Cool!' His life was so EPIC! He had always liked being popular; he was so popular that even his teachers appreciated him. Everyone respected him like he was their principal, and his coolness gave him privileges. For instance, he'd often get to sit in the teacher's spinning chair while the other students looked on. After each lesson, it felt like every kid in Mattyiene's class would crowd around him. They would listen to everything he had to say and cheer on his every word, like fans cheering for their favourite celebrity. So, now you can understand how popular he was, right???

Our 11-year-old king was as popular as Nike 270s!!! Everyone loved him, all except the school's weirdo, Nerdy Nero...

I will tell you about Nero in a minute, but I ask that you be patient. That's because first, I will describe Mattyiene's family.

The Bolt family:

Mattyiene lives with his 8–year-old brother, Ike, his mum, Shanique, and his dad, Andre. To Mattyiene, his brother was a pain. Ike was the most animated and geeky kid ever, and he had a mouth to go with it. He was short for his age but made up for it with attitude. He was proud of the fact that he had the coolest brother for miles and in his head thought they were similar. There is a picture of Ike below.

Did you know that Ike means 'brings laughter' in Hebrew? Mattyiene suspected that Ike got his name cause his parents were pleased that Ike was born. Mattyiene wanted to know the origin of his name, but every time he asked, he was told that no one knows! Mattyiene concluded he couldn't have brought that much joy to his parents upon his arrival, which explained a lot.

His middle name was Zachary, so just maybe his parents had given some thought to that name. He needed to do some research to check, but he never seemed to get around to it. Mattyiene noted that their parents paid close attention to Ike whenever he was talking. They called him nick-names like 'Shine of my Shoes.' And 'Pride of my Basket.' Mattyiene had concluded a long time ago he would have to make his name count and that with a name like Mattyiene Zachary Bolt, he had to deliver. "Being cool" was a good place to start.

"Mattyiene Zachary Bolt, yeah! I'm proud of my name, and that my family live in England and I attend this really leng school!" Leng? When asked what leng meant, Mat-tyiene would reply, "Just means leng! Good!" OK Mattyiene was stretching it. It actually means extremely attractive; good looking, but it was a word he found cool so used at every opportunity.

-

2

CHAPTER TWO: TOO COOL FOR SCHOOL!!

Mattyiene's mother Shanique leaned across the kitchen counter and took a piece of his toast. She shuffled around to the boys with her hands full, juggling her bag,thermos cup, and a book. Shanique was an athletic woman who looked younger than her years. She always had energy, despite her job and the responsibility of having two young children.

She kissed the boys and headed for the front door, rushing so she didn't miss her train to work. Her hair was neatly braided, plaited in a ponytail at the back of her head, and tied with a bright coloured scarf. On the whole, Mattyiene thought his mum was chilled and nerdy, but cool. She wasn't strict, but when her children misbehaved, she would lay down the law. "Andre! Please make sure these children get to school on time. Love ya!" Shanique shouted as she closed

the door behind her. Soon after, Andre strolled in dressed for work. He was wearing a cool two- piece tracksuit and

5

a pair of trainers that Mattyiene hoped he would Will to him if he happened to leave this earth. He wore his hair in a ponytail. Andre looked like he had missed something. "Where is your mum?" He asked. The boys looked at each other in confusion. "She went to work and told us you will be taking us to school," they replied to their father.

Andre grabbed a bottle of water from the fridge and told the boys to grab their stuff. Andre was a cheerful man but somewhat forgetful. Despite his busy schedule, he always did things positively. Like his wife, he was not strict with his children unless they took things too far.

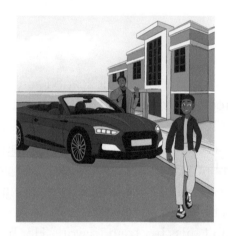

They arrived at Mattyiene's school in dad's BMW 5 Series Convertible after dropping Ike off first. Dad loved his car and always seemed relieved when they got out of his car without leaving a mess behind. He shouted to Mattyiene that he should get a lift back home after school with his friend Deyonte's parents, who lived two doors down from them.

It was a beautiful day, and the sun was shining brightly in the English sky, lighting up the mighty school building.

The school was as large as a mansion. But as colossal as it was, the windows were always gleaming, the massive lawns were trimmed, and the high wooden beam walls had a constant whiff of polish. Even the birds knew not to drop their you-know-what on the Windows!

In the morning, there were three bells. The first bell told the students that school was open. The second bell was a warning to get to class, and if you weren't settled by that third bell, detention!!!

The principal of the school was a Ghanaian woman called Miss Kyla, who was proud of her school. She was determined to have the best school in the city. Miss Kyla had her hair in an afro that always looked immaculate. Her dress sense was quirky but smart. She wore bright-coloured suits with suede pumps. She loved her school and students and wanted them to be properly educated. She knew everyone by name and knew their parents. Once Mattyiene told her his ultra-ambitious wish for life, she didn't even flinch. She just responded, "Let's get that plan in action."

Mattyiene swaggered through the corridor with an air of self-importance wafting off of him. As he headed for class, the usual invitation of a fist pump came Mattyiene's way. He casually waved back at lots of other children. In his head, he thought back to the extraordinary night before. He had been playing an online game called *GENIUS WORLD*. The game was educational (Now, for sure you think it's boring. Well, you're not alone, but we've got to learn somehow! And it's the only way my parents will allow me to stay on gaming). The aim of the game was to answer as many math questions as possible. You might think, "easy peasy. " Well, there is a catch - you only have two minutes to answer the questions.

Mattyiene was a legend at the game. But as you `might expect, he played the game with a good dose of cool, so now other children were signing on to play.

Anyway, our math master, Mattyiene, was having a party at a skateboard park the week after next. He planned on showing his friends his epic skateboard moves. He opened the creaky door of his classroom, slunk into his seat, and opened his English book to page 8. That was the chapter his class was supposed to read and answer questions about, but it looked like he was the only one doing any work. The others were chattering, sniggering, and generally avoiding the chapter! Mattyiene liked English but kept that quiet for fear of appearing nerdy.

See, Mattyiene was a very smart boy for his age, but he thought that being popular was more important than intelligence.

At that moment, he realised it was not the best time to give out his party invites because he really wanted an audience when he gave them out. He specifically had no intention of inviting Jeremiah, who was still struggling to acknowledge Mattyiene's cool status. Jeremiah had caused Mattyiene's embarrassment more than once, like the day he put a sign on Mattyiene's back calling him a loser. So, now was not the time. He didn't have their full attention, so he thought he would try again tomorrow.

After school, Mattyiene visited the local skateboard park. Just him with his board; the park was empty. Between you and me, this was because the rest of his class was in detention for lack of work! But this worked for Mattyiene, and you will see why in a moment.

Mattyiene put his board at the edge of the ramp and went sliding down. Forgetting what he was doing, he thought back to his perfect score on the amazing *GENIUS WORLD* scoreboard, where he was top and the amazing presentation that he had given three weeks ago on the Earth's Crust. Those memories could not rescue him from the catastrophe that was playing out in front his very eyes, with him at centre stage. Suddenly, his arms went flailing all around and he then landed headfirst on the concrete ground. A stream of blood came gushing from his left palm as he skidded on the ground. To his horror, he realised he couldn't skate... maybe he needed to hold back on those invites until he had sorted out this problem.

3

CHAPTER THREE: TWO COOL FOR SCHOOL

Nero, a skinny boy with Brown, limp hair, was very irate with the cool kids for ignoring him. What did he have to do to get a notice? A spontaneous fist pump would be cool. Often, he felt miserable for being such a nerd and so uncool. He constantly plotted how to avoid school. Nero was a very studious boy, but he was not good at chatting and socialising with other children. So, this boy spent most of his days at the skateboard park where you could zoom about with little or no encounters with other kids - he was very good at skateboarding, and it was one of his specialties. He was a damn good skater. Yes!! But on a COOL KID scale, from 1-10, Nero rated a zero. This did not add up. In his head nerd did not normally equal good skater. His group of friends were all nerdy like him and they could just about walk let alone skate. He was an anomaly. But maybe, just maybe not all cool kids could skate! Maybe he had a cool zone that Mattyiene could only dream of.

CHAPTER FOUR: BROTHERLY LOVE

So, Ike thought he was as cool as his brother... which as far from true. He was

as cool as a newborn baby.

"Hi, it's Ike. Even though it's my brother's story, I thought I should introduce myself.

I am Mattyiene's younger brother; unlike Mattyiene, my name means something! My name means "brings laughter," by the way. I am as cool as my bro. Super cool. I always want to go out with him and his friends so we can all be cool together.

But it never happens...

Whatever Mattyiene can do, I can do it better. Here is my golden opportunity; here he comes. So, please tell him how cool you think I am. Bye!"

Without Mattyiene noticing, Ike followed him out of the house. It was only when Ike turned the corner he realised his uncool brother was following him.

"Where do you think you're going? " Mattyiene asked Ike and sent him home. As he was walking home, Ike thought, "we still have a lot in common."

But did they? Did they really? Well, all they had in common was their parents, both boys, and they were both black. That's it!

4

CHAPTER FIVE: FROM ZEROS TO HEROES

Remember Miss Kyla, who had red, rainbow hair? She was Mattyiene's headteacher and wanted her school to be the best school in the city. The weird thing about Miss Kyla was that she was a clean freak. She made sure the students washed their hands twice before sitting down every lesson. She was really just that fastidious.

She also thought that all of her students loved her. "I rule as a head," she would sing to herself. So, in her head, her students were crazy about her. "The kids think I'm perfect!" She also sang out. But she wondered, "why do I find booby traps all around my office? "

The school motto was very important to her. The children sang it out loud every day. The motto was:
DETERMINATION
INDEPENDENCE
TEAMWORK

NEVER GIVE UP
WE ARE FIGHTERS
WE ARE WARRIORS

At this point, you might think it is a truly pretentious motto. But the truth is that Miss Kyla made it because she thought the children were like bundles of misery, needing all the help she could give. "I need to get these bundles of misery up to scratch," she would think. She thought her school needed to have a nice sensitive head teacher, but she also wondered if that was the most effective way and maybe a harsher approach might just knock these kids into shape. All in all, she was a very peculiar woman. Part strict and part obsessive, but at the same time, she had a certain joy in her manner.

For now, we will leave the headteacher alone and return to our hero.

After school, Mattyiene was in his bedroom. He was thinking back to the day he

fell off his skateboard and realised he couldn't skate. "What can I do?? " He wondered.

Mattyiene strongly wanted to learn to skate - there was no way that a cool kid couldn't even do a stunt.

Mattyiene needed to learn to skate. Mattyiene thought of all the good skaters at his school. Sadly, and ironically, they were all Nero's friends. It was a very ironic situation. At that moment he thought: "OH NO!! I HAVE TO BE FRIENDS WITH NERDY NERO, WITH HIS NERDY CONTAGIOUS- NESS. I wonder if there is another way. OH, MAN! I'd rather smell my dog's breath. "

He felt devastated.

5

CHAPTER SIX: LET THE GAMES BEGIN

To Nero, his life was like a recurring video game, but he was the only player. At

school, it was playtime and Mattyiene walked out into the playground. He looked at the chain-link fence in the corner of the playground. He also looked at the monkey bars, where Nero and his friends were hanging out. Nero was pretending to be Superman by hanging on a bar with one hand. Mattyiene remembered he had to be friends with Nero, so he quickly dashed along the pavement until he was just behind him.

Instantly, Nero's friends fled. Nero's cheeks were turning light red, and he was anxious about being alone with Mattyiene. He thought, why is he here? "Do you want to play a game with my friends and me? " Mattyiene asked nervously but trying to remain cool.

When Nero heard that proposal, he thought it was a joke at first. He spent a few long seconds staring at Mattyiene's face, until he answered, "Yes please!" He was smiling, big time. Nero followed the cool kid, feeling curious but happy. Mattyiene's friends groaned and muttered under their breath as Nero slunk in with them, but he just ignored their blank looks.

6

CHAPTER SEVEN: PLAY DATES WITH NEW MATES

I can't count the number of excuses Mattyiene gave Nero to get out of

Going skating. The first step had been taken, and they were now getting to know each other.

Fortunately, Nero always wanted to skate, as that was his true passion.

It was four p.m. , a beautiful sunny spring day, after school. Nero and his new buddy were walking up a hill that was so high you could camp on it. They started talking about their lives for the first time. Mattyiene started to realise that Nero was not the loser he had always believed...

The next day, they went skating. Mattyiene approached the ramp in the skate park. Nero was

showing him how to do a kick-turn but not expecting Mattyiene to do this for now. Nero took his board, and down he went. His Brown hay-like hair flapped in the cold breeze. Nero landed on his board like his feet were glued tight onto it. Mattyiene tried next. He cleared his mind so he could focus, and then he went to the curved bit of the ramp. Mattyiene steered his board by leaning it towards the direction he wanted to go to. He wanted to go left. As he steered the board, he carefully landed.

"Wow! Nice one, dude! " Nero told Mattyiene.

He was very impressed.

7

CHAPTER EIGHT: ON A MISSION TO SKATE!!

Later on, Mattyiene and Nero were skateboarding home. Mattyiene was getting
better at skating, just as Nero had said. Even Mattyiene was proud that Nero had taught him to skateboard. As they approached Nero's house, Mattyiene tried to do the Ollie, apparently the simplest skateboard trick there is. (Well, he has to learn one of these days, right?) He has seen this trick on YouTube, where, of course, he was popular.

Sadly, fellow readers, our friend Mattyiene stood on the curved bit of the
skateboard and fell over backwards. Unfortunately, he was not prepared for such a challenge, and the skateboard rolled into a dark alley.

Suddenly, a little figure appeared through the shadows. Mattyiene or Nero couldn't make out who the little figure was, but it took the board and ran back through the gloomy shadows, laughing like the world's most sarcastic clown.

"Hey!" Mattyiene shouted, running into the shadows.

"Someone's up to antics," Mattyiene told Nero sadly.

"You're right, my friend," Nero replied quietly. " Let's look for it tomorrow!" Nero suddenly exclaimed. Mattyiene nodded solemnly, as he scowled back towards the area where his board had been taken.

8

CHAPTER NINE: QUESTIONS

The next day, Mattyiene woke up early. He got dressed, had a tasty snack, and then went back onto the street. As soon as people came his way, he immediately started to ask them questions about where his board might be.

No one knew any facts. When he got home, he started questioning his own family.

His Mom and Dad made it quite obvious that they had no idea where the board was, but Ike was being very strange.

"I don't know where it is. Why are you asking me? I am not a thief," he protested.

Mattyiene thought his brother was being very suspicious.

"We'll see." He muttered under his breath.

The next morning, when Ike was at his friend's house, Mattyiene searched his

room. He looked at his medals and posters. He looked under his bed, behind shelves, and even inside his cabinet.

Mattyiene began to trash his brothers' room, muttering things about Ike under his breath.

"That little... F.E.D. stole my board."

When Ike got home, his room looked like the inside of a rubbish bin.

"Who did this?! " He raged.

"If you tell me who took my skateboard, I will tell you who trashed your room," Mattyiene replied, leaning on the side of his door.

-

9

CHAPTER TEN: FROM IKE'S PERSPECTIVE

"Why would I know where your board is, genius?" Ike replied.

"I know you took it! " Mattyiene, filled with anger, shouted at Ike.

"You thief! "

"At least my name has meaning," Ike responded.

"Yeah, and at least I am cool, and you are not," Mattyiene said to his brother. It was sad for Ike to hear that, but it was a terrible truth. He was a F.E.D!

Without another word, Ike scurried down the stairs. Later on, the boy's parents told both boys to apologise. After they had a sort of lame stare off, they did.

Now, dear readers, we will see the situation from the younger brother's perspective.

"Hi, it's Ike again. I know I keep busting in, but why would I want my brother's board? It's not like he's cool and I'm not - then I might want his board. Wait, do you readers think I'm cool? Do you? Yes!! Let's go! I didn't take his stupid board.

But just confirming, he did mess up my room, right?"

"Ike... Ike, where are you hiding? "

"He's coming; got to go. Bye again."

-

10

CHAPTER ELEVEN:
BUSTED!

Nero came to meet Mattyiene at his house the next day. He showed his friend a page of a fake newspaper that said that the skateboard had been found.

COOL KID'S SKATEBOARD FOUND IN PARK
RECOGNISED BY COOL KID'S FRIEND.
THIEF DROPPED IT
NO CLUE WHO TOOK IT
INVESTIGATORS ARE UP TO SCRATCH

SO, IF YOU ARE THE COOL KID, COME GET YOUR SKATEBOARD... Both thought it strange but went with it.

"This page is plastered all over the place. Someone is playing a prank on you! " Nero said, somewhat excited. Mattyiene replied to Nero that they needed to find his board and the criminal mastermind behind this whole thing. The fake newspaper said the skateboard was found in a colossal park, the most popular park in England. To them, the colossal park had to be their local park, so they went looking. Mattyiene and Nero searched for the board and studied the fake newspaper announcement for clues about where the skateboard could be, but they got no answers. They were tired and it was getting dark.

Behind a tree, a little figure grinned to himself. "We'll see who's cooler." He told himself slyly. As you might have guessed, the little figure was Ike.

"That's it! I can't take this anymore." Mattyiene suddenly shouted. He pulled his phone out of his pocket. He was going to call Ike to get himself and Nero out of this disaster. When Mattyiene called Ike, a vibration sounded instantly. Behind that same tree, Ike ran past with Mattyiene's board in his hands.

At that moment, he began to run. Despite being smaller, he was faster than his brother.

"It was my stupid brother who stole my board! " Mattyiene told Nero, breathless when Ike had run out of sight.

"So, your brother is going to be exposed, big time!" Nero replied.

-

CHAPTER TWELVE: THE TRUTH

When Mattyiene told his parents that Ike stole his skateboard, they refused to listen to him!!

"It's true, I swear. You can even ask Nerdy... I mean, you can even ask Nero." He tried to tell them.

"You guys have been spending a lot of time playing together. Is he your friend?" questioned Mattyiene's dad.

"Don't change the subject. We are discussing my F.E.D. brother stealing my skateboard."

Just then, Ike came in and bellowed at the top of his lungs, "WHY WOULD I TAKE YOUR SKATEBOARD! ? "

"You did, Dr. Uncool!" Mattyiene shouted.

The boy's parents didn't know who to believe. Should they believe Mattyiene because he looked so serious and upset with Ike? Or should they believe their eight-year-old favourite child, who, in their opinion, barely lied?

"EVERYONE STOP SHOUTING!" said mum.

"One of you is lying but we don't know who it is," their dad said as if it wasn't

obvious.

"You don't say," Mattyiene snapped at once.

"Watch your tone or I will ground you for a month!"

Mattyiene scoffed.

"I'll make it a year!"

"Fine," Mattyiene said

"That's going to be two years," his dad said, raising his voice

"Thanks," Mattyiene shouted as he slammed his bed-room door closed.

"Three years it is," his dad finished, chuckling to himself.

That night was very weird, as the brothers scowled at each other at dinner as their parents discussed who might be lying. Before Mattyiene went to bed, his parents said to him in a gentle voice.

"We know you are..."

In Mattyiene's head, he guessed what they were going to say.

"Telling the truth... telling the truth, "He thought in his head.

"... lying!" They finished.

"But I'm..."His father cut him off and told him never to lie. For the rest of the night, Mattyiene was too angry to sleep. He got out of bed, went to his brother's room, and opened the door a little bit. His brother was in his bed and his back was turned. The 'too cool for school' kid tiptoed into the room using a minuscule torch he had gotten for Christmas. He aimed the torch at his brother in bed only to realise it was all his brother's toys, arranged to make it look like his legs were in bed, and a mask to make it look like his head was there. Mattyiene thought his brother was annoying, but he still cared about him. (Wouldn't you? Be honest with yourself.)

Mattyiene didn't hesitate. He ran downstairs and saw a note.

The note read:

"If you read this, my cool brother, I just want you to know

That I want to be cooler, so I have run away with your skateboard, so you'll fail at your party

Hahahahahahahahahahahaha! I will come home when I feel like it.

If you tell mum and dad, you're finished!

From your bro, Ike. "

Mattyiene scowled.

-

12

CHAPTER THIRTEEN: CLUES

At this point, you're probably wondering what Ike's motives were for treating his brother in this way. Was he jealous of his brother's popularity? Or was he a problem child but intelligent at the same time? The truth is that both statements were correct.

Well, after this little reflection, it is time to go back to our story.

Even though it was nearly six o'clock in the morning, Mattyiene tried to call Ike. But Ike wasn't stupid, and he knew that Mattyiene had already put a tracking device on his phone.

Why would he take the phone? Mattyiene would find him too easily that way. Sudden vibration sounded from behind the sofa - Ike's phone was ringing. Mattyiene ended the call. Despite the huge differences he had with his brother, he was worried about him. After all, he was just a young boy and had run away from home in the middle of the night. Disillusioned and nervous, he began to think of another plan when suddenly his cell phone rang. It was none other than the Nerd of the school, Nerdy Nero.

"Dude, I think I just saw your brother running down the lane opposite my HOUSE!!!" He told Mattyiene as he feared for the worst.

"Yeah," Mattyiene said solemnly, "he also left me a note."

They agreed to meet each other at *COOL BROS NACHOS*, which was a

restaurant opposite Nero's house. By the way, *Nachos* are a Mexicali dish made in America from Mexican ingredients. To make them, you:

1. Get some tortillas
2. Cut them into small triangles and fry them
3. Fry them in one gallon of corn oil at 175°C
4. Cover them with cheese (and any other topics you like, like onions, jalapeños, or corn) and bake them in an oven for about ten minutes
5. Wait 1-2 mins for them to cool down
6. Fill a few separate bowls with dips like guacamole, salsa, and sour cream

7. Another good topping would be cooked and seasoned mince, which you could put on at the same time as the cheese. (What do you mean, you already knew that? I was just saying. GEEZ!)
8. Now stuff your face with the food!

At this point in the book, you may be wondering why Ike is being such a weird brother.

Why is he doing all of this? Is he jealous of how cool his bro is? Is he trying to copy that?

Coolness by taking the skateboard. Who knows? Nobody, that's who!

WELL... except me, obviously.

When Mattyiene met Nero outside the shop, Nero looked like he had wrestled an alligator and a bear at the same time. He looked a mess. He had just jumped out of bed and pulled his clothes on.

"So where did my..."- But Nero interrupted him.

"He told me that you aren't really my friend and that you're just pretending so you can learn to skateboard to look cooler in front of your friends. Is that true?" Nero asked, deeply irritated.

"What are you, the newest cop of this century? Of course, I am your friend. Name one reason why you would believe my brother!" Mattyiene challenged.

Between you and me, that's where the trouble really started.

13

CHAPTER FOURTEEN: ROASTED!

"Well firstly," Nero begun. "You have never played with me or even talked to me until a few

weeks ago."

"Well steady on, Mr. Hurt Feelings, but maybe if you weren't so nerdy you would

have more friends."

"Ok, let's see how this nerd is at roasting," Nero said. " You want a roasting

competition? "

"Easy, you're insulting my intelligence. I'll start. I'll start," Mattyiene replied.

"Ok!" Nero shouted.

"You've got blue shoes," Mattyiene said.

Nero looked at him with pity in his eyes as he scoffed a piece of dry toast."

"I think your next meal should be a dictionary." Nero boomed.

"Your next meal should be a packet of coolness," Mattyiene said, wincing at his own terrible
comeback.

"You have the brain of an amoeba," Nero said simply.

"You're so dumb; when the teacher told you 2+2=4, you probably asked. '4 what?' "

"You're so ugly, when you were born the doctor was blinded, so he slapped your
mum, then he took a second look and slapped your dad!" Nero responded, winning
the challenge.

"Well... well... well, I'm sorry. I just wanted to learn how to skateboard."

"Well, you could have just asked me; I would have helped you." Nero replied softly
but seriously.

"Do you want to come to my birthday party on Friday?" Mattyiene asked his friend
after they had apologised with a fist pump.

"Yeah, of course! " Nero shouted with joy.

"Coolio!"

14

CHAPTER FIFTEEN: THE END!

Mattyiene's party went really well - just like this book. In the end, Mattyiene

proved that cool boys have problems, too, including looking a little awkward in this picture. I love cake but its lame having to sit in front of the cake, contemplating blowing out candles, with a bunch of people watching. Anyway, you might be wondering what happened between Ike and Mattyiene. Well, our hero finally captured the elusive little boy near Nero's house. Fortunately, he and the skateboard were fine.

When they returned home, Ike had to follow his brother's instructions and write lines that read: "I am not cool at all if I steal or run away from home" 50 times a day. That was a just and necessary punishment for Ike, the boy who was supposed to bring laughter.

So, dear readers, I sincerely hope that this book has taught you that nerds can be friends with cool kids and vice-versa. Intelligence and popularity do not have to be opposites. Miss Kyla became fun, and she was not only a principal but she also became a PE teacher. Mattyiene and Ike explained what had happened to the skateboard, to the humiliation of Ike and vindication of Mattyiene.

Dear readers, I sincerely hope you enjoyed reading this book as much as I did writing it. See ya until we meet again!

THE END!!!

© Malachi Williams 2021

CPSIA information can be obtained
at www.ICGtesting.com
Printed in the USA
BVHW060023190123
656592BV00001B/2